GAME ON!

EYES ON THE PUCK

BY BRANDON TERRELL

STORY
LIBRARY

www.12StoryLibrary.com

12-Story Library is an imprint of Peterson Publishing Company
and Press Room Editions.

Produced for 12-Story Library by Red Line Editorial

Photographs ©: iStockphoto, cover

Cover Design: Nikki Farinella

ISBN
978-1-63235-048-0 (hardcover)
978-1-63235-108-1 (paperback)
978-1-62143-089-6 (hosted ebook)

Library of Congress Control Number: 2014946009

Printed in the United States of America
Mankato, MN
October, 2014

TABLE OF CONTENTS

CHAPTER 1

THE WALL

Annie Roger slapped her hockey stick against the ice and loudly shouted, "Come on, Grizzlies!" She watched from her position in front of the goal as the other players took their places for the first face-off of the season. Ruby Vogel, East Grover Lake's tall center, skated to center ice and came to a quick stop. She surveyed her teammates like a general admiring her troops before battle.

She looked back at Annie. The two locked eyes, and Ruby nodded.

Annie slapped her stick on the ice again in return. She was ready.

The crowd cheered, with the loudest cheers coming from just above the Grizzlies' bench, on the other side of the thick Plexiglas barrier. Annie saw her friends Ben Mason, Logan Parrish, and Gabe Santiago waving their arms and rooting for the Grizzlies. Logan was even wearing a ridiculous red foam finger that said "WE'RE #1!" and a hat shaped like a bear head.

Only Logan, Annie thought, shaking her head. He always liked to goof around.

Sitting next to Logan, Annie saw Carter Cressman. Carter was new to Grover Lake Middle School. He had started spending more and more time with Annie and her friends, something Annie didn't mind. Not one single bit. Carter wore a heavy winter coat. His hands were tucked into his pockets. His black hair swooped over his forehead. Annie's heart skipped a beat.

Oh man, I didn't realize Carter would be watching me play.

Of course, it was pretty obvious why Carter was at the game, when Annie thought about it. His dad *was* the team's new coach, the reason Carter had transferred here.

Annie took a deep breath and muttered to herself, "No distractions. Focus."

The ref blew his whistle and dropped the puck. The game was officially underway.

Ruby slashed at the puck, knocking it back to the Grizzlies' left wing, Naya Jessen. She brought the puck across the blue line and into the attacking zone.

The Grizzlies' opponents, the Rhinehart Rockets, had a set of tall, imposing twins on defense. One of them met Naya head-on and slapped the puck away before she could get off a shot.

Ruby tracked down the puck and brought it back across the blue line. She passed to Heidi Gordon, the right winger, who had an open shot. Heidi brought her stick high and smacked the puck hard. It sizzled through the air but was deflected by the goalie.

Ruby was there for the rebound. With a flick of her wrist, she perfectly placed her shot over the goalie's left shoulder. It hit the back of the net.

The red light behind the goal whirled and a siren sounded, signaling the goal.

"Goal!" Annie shouted, her voice muffled by both her mouthguard and her visored mask.

After the Grizzlies' quick score, the two teams settled in. The Rockets' best left wing was a girl named Bryn Larson. She was remarkably good, and she wasn't afraid to take a shot. Annie kept her eyes on Bryn. Once, still early in the game, Bryn took a wrist shot that blazed toward the corner of the goal, but Annie deflected it with her leg pad. Another time, Bryn tried a slap shot in front of the goal, but Annie knocked it away with her blocker.

Her teammates nicknamed Annie "The Wall" because hardly anything got by her.

As the end of the first period was winding down, the Grizzlies were still up 1-0. Ruby brought the puck up the ice and across the blue line. As she lined up a shot, the puck was stripped away by one of the twin Rocket defensive players. She passed up to their center. The center passed it over to Bryn, who immediately shot the puck.

The puck looked a little fuzzy to Annie as it sailed high, past a Grizzlies defensive player. But Annie easily caught it in her oversized glove, called a trapper.

The ref stopped play.

Piece of cake, she thought one moment, and then next, *that was a little weird*, thinking about how the puck looked fuzzy to her.

As Annie passed the puck to the ref, Ruby skated past. "Nice save," she said.

Annie nodded and slapped her stick on the ice. Then she waited for the ensuing face-off.

CHAPTER 2

COLLISION

Second period: 1-0.

Annie liked seeing that goose egg up on the scoreboard.

Before the start of the second period, Annie lumbered out to the goal. Her skates were different than the rest of the team's. Her blades were wider and flatter, giving her more stability on the ice. The boots were more rigid as well, which made it hard to turn sharply.

The Rockets won the face-off to start the second period. Their center quickly brought the puck into the Grizzlies' defending zone. Annie watched it fly between Rockets like a bullet as they passed it back and forth. It was a blur sliding across the ice. In the locker room, between periods, their coach must have told them to move the puck around, trying to use misdirection to fool Annie.

Not against The Wall, she thought.

The two defensive players on the Grizzlies' first line, Piper and Britney, danced around, making sure the Rockets didn't get a clean shot. Finally, their right wing attempted a wrist shot. Annie nearly lost sight of the puck as it glanced off Britney's skate and almost ricocheted in. At the last second, Annie shot her leg out and blocked it. Then she dropped both hands over the loose puck.

Tweet!

"Face-off," the ref said.

Ruby took the dropped puck and sent it skittering around the boards, behind the net, to a waiting Piper. Piper fired the puck up into the neutral zone, and the Rockets' players cleared out.

Annie watched as Naya took the puck into the Rocket's defensive zone. Then she flicked the puck to Ruby, who fired a quick wrist shot. But the shot was deflected by the Rockets' goalie.

"Watch it!" Coach Cressman shouted from the bench as two girls tangled along the boards for the puck. The Rockets came away with it and quickly passed it up to Bryn.

There was no one between her and the goal, except Annie. Bryn had a clear breakaway, and she skated furiously across the blue line. Annie steadied herself. She took a deep, calming breath.

Concentrate on the puck, not the player, she reminder herself. It didn't matter what fancy moves Bryn tried to execute. Annie's attention was on the black disk currently zipping down the ice in her direction. But she was having trouble focusing on it.

"You got this, Annie!" Carter shouted. Annie nearly turned to the stands to see him watching her.

No! Focus!

From nowhere, Piper rushed up from behind to meet Bryn. The speedy Rocket tried to swerve around the approaching defensive player, but couldn't. The two girls tangled, their sticks clashing. Piper lost hers, and it spun across the ice, striking the far board hard.

The two girls tripped and fell to the ice. Their momentum, however, propelled them forward. The ref blew his whistle, and the rest of the players came to a stop.

Piper and Bryn slid right toward Annie.

Annie needed to get out of the way. But as she looked across the ice at the approaching players, she had to squint to see them clearly.

Whoa. That's weird.

She shook her head to clear her vision, but by then it was too late. The tangled hockey players slid into Annie, knocking her legs out from under her. She flew into the air.

Then the side of her mask connected with the ice

Crack!

Stars lit up Annie's vision as she landed in a heap inside the net. When she opened her eyes, she saw the puck lying just past the red line of the goal.

"Doesn't . . . count . . ." she whispered. *The whistle blew, stopping play.*

Annie tried to sit up, and she could hear Bryn and Piper groaning and doing the same. Piper said something like, "You all right?"

Annie tried to answer, but she felt woozy. Everything looked fuzzy.

"Coach Cressman! I think Annie's hurt!" Piper yelled out.

DAZED BUT DETERMINED

"Annie, just stay where you are."

Coach Cressman knelt beside Annie, who was still sitting on the ice. She looked up at Coach. He wore a Grizzlies ball cap and had chiseled features. *Carter looks so much like him*, Annie thought. His face was serious, as if set in stone.

"I'm okay, Coach, really," Annie said. And she was. At least, she felt that way. Her vision was normal again. She felt a little sore, but she'd taken worse hits.

Annie sat up stiffly. Coach Cressman placed a hand on her back to help, and then offered her his other arm as leverage. Getting to her feet was a slow process, one that made Annie feel like a turtle who'd been turned on her shell and needed help righting herself.

The crowd clapped when they saw that Annie was okay. She waved weakly and started to skate toward the bench.

She saw her parents and younger sister, Olivia, standing and watching her nervously. Her mother chewed at her fingernails, a bad habit she never could quite break. Annie's friends had moved down to the front row, right behind the bench. They all looked concerned, especially Carter.

"Annie, are you okay?" Ben asked as she walked along the rubberized floor of the bench and took a seat.

She nodded. "I'm ready to get back out there."

"Not happening." Coach Cressman had overheard her. "Emma, you're in."

Emma Radley was Annie's backup. Emma was decent, but she was nowhere as fast with her glove as Annie.

Annie tried one more time. "Coach," she said, "I can totally go in."

Coach Cressman glanced at her but said nothing. He only shook his head.

Annie could do nothing but watch as the Grizzlies and the Rockets faced off again. The Rockets were in a power play, thanks to Piper tripping Bryn. Piper was in the penalty box on the far side of the rink, sitting for two minutes.

The Rockets took advantage of the five-on-four power play and attacked the zone. Annie could almost see the panic on Emma's face as she whipped her head left and right, trying to follow the puck. She couldn't keep up, though, and one of the Rocket wings slapped a shot right past her.

The siren blew and the light twirled.

Tie game.

Annie clenched her fists together in her lap but held her tongue.

In the third period, the Rockets added two more goals. Ruby was able to sneak a shot into the net, too, but it wasn't enough.

The Grizzlies lost by a score of 3-2.

As they skated off the ice, Annie heard Emma mumble, "Sorry, guys."

"No apologizing," Coach Cressman said. "The Rockets are a good team. You played well."

"Thanks, Coach," Emma said, still mumbling.

Annie's family was waiting with the rest of the Grizzlies' parents by the concession stand as she stepped out of the locker room. Her parents were speaking with Coach Cressman. *Probably about my fall*, Annie thought. Her sister, Olivia, looked cold and ready to leave. Annie's friends stood nearby.

Annie lugged her equipment bag, a giant duffel that was extremely cumbersome. It weighed heavily on her shoulder.

She walked over to her friends and dropped the equipment bag to the floor with a loud *whump*. "Hey," was all she could muster to say. She wasn't going to unleash her frustration about the situation. Not here, where other parents and players were standing around.

"How are you feeling?" Ben asked her.

She shrugged. "Fine." Then she added under her breath so only the guys could hear, "I totally could have gone back into the game."

"Annie . . ." Ben began to protest.

"I could have easily stopped those goals. You *know* I could have. I mean, I'm *way* better than Emma."

Her volume had increased as she spoke, and she realized that other people could hear her. She felt bad dissing Emma, and she looked around to make sure no one was glaring at her.

Thankfully, no one was.

"Sorry you got hurt," Carter said. "That sucks."

She looked down and blushed at his concern.

"Annie, you have to listen to your coach," Gabe said. He was the reasonable, cautious one in their group.

"Yeah, I know."

She glanced over and saw her dad shaking Coach Cressman's hand. Then the coach came over and placed a hand on Carter's shoulder. "Thanks for cheering us on, boys," he said with a tired smile. Then, to Annie, he added, "Take it easy for a couple of days, Annie." Carter said his goodbyes, and then the two walked up the stairs and out of the ice rink.

Annie's parents and sister soon joined the foursome. Her dad picked the equipment bag up off the floor and slung it over his shoulder. Her mom asked, "How is . . . well, how are you?" She was looking at Annie as if she were a time bomb that needed to be defused.

"I'm fine," Annie answered. "Can we go home, please?"

"Sure thing," her dad said.

Annie said goodbye to her friends and followed her parents out of the ice rink and into the blustery, cold afternoon.

CHAPTER 4

SEEING THINGS

On their way home from the rink, Annie's mom, concerned for her daughter's well-being, called their family doctor and made an appointment for the following morning.

"Just to be safe," she said.

So before she went to school, Annie was forced to sit beside her mom in the doctor's waiting room. As they waited for Dr. Norris, Annie grew quite worried.

What if I'm actually hurt? What if I have a concussion or something and Dr. Norris says I can't play hockey the rest of the season?

She fidgeted around in her white plastic seat. She hadn't told anyone about how she'd momentarily lost sight of the two girls rushing toward her on the ice.

I'm sure it's nothing, she tried to reassure herself.

Right?

Suddenly, Annie was very annoyed at how childishly the pediatrician's office was decorated. It was as if a unicorn had exploded and showered rainbow-colored guts all over the place.

Ugh. Get me out of here. Quick.

As it turned out, Annie had nothing to worry about. Dr. Norris, the slender, older pediatrician who had been Annie's doc since she was a newborn, gave her the all clear to play. "Just try not to overdo it, young lady," he advised her as he handed her the small basket filled with suckers. "Maybe sit out a couple of games, just until you feel one hundred percent."

Annie, as tough as she acted, was still a sucker for . . . well, for suckers. She plucked a strawberry one out of the mix.

"Sure thing, Doc," she lied.

Sitting on the sidelines was not something Annie particularly enjoyed. And she wasn't going to give up her spot as starting goalie easily. She felt fine, and Dr. Norris had said she was healthy.

Before they left, Dr. Norris said to her mom, "You might want to make an appointment with an optometrist . . ."

Annie was too busy unwrapping her sucker to listen.

Annie saw nothing wrong with suiting up after school the following day for practice. As she walked into the locker room at the rink, many of the other players were already there.

Ruby Vogel, in uniform and taping up her stick, looked happy to see her. Some of the other girls looked surprised. Piper looked happy. A mix of relief and disappointment washed over Emma's face.

"I'm so glad you're okay," she said as Annie sat down beside her on the wooden bench.

"Never felt better," Annie said with a smile.

Coach Cressman didn't seem as convinced. "We'll take it easy on you to start," he said, arms crossed, as Annie prepared to take the ice.

The team started by skating laps around the rink. Annie watched them as she stretched. She loved the sound of skates skittering across the ice. It made her adrenaline surge, her pulse quicken.

After the team had warmed up, they ran a couple of drills. One for passing. Another for skating. And one for shooting.

Annie crouched and prepared to defend the goal as the first wave of three players wove down the ice, passing the puck back and forth. It was the Grizzlies' first line offense: Ruby, Naya, and Heidi. When it was time to shoot, Heidi was the one who flicked a wrist shot at Annie.

She snagged it out of the air, and tossed it back onto the ice.

See? I'm totally fine.

The next trio of players made their way toward the goal. Annie squinted, and for the briefest moment, she lost focus. She scrambled to find the puck and was just able to pick it up before the wing fired a shot. Annie deflected it with her blocker.

What was that?

Then, as the third line came toward her, she lost sight of the puck entirely. It was just a black blob on the ice. She squinted as best she could, but could *barely* make it out.

And then . . .

It zipped right past her, into the net.

"Nice shot, Lexie!" Coach Cressman shouted.

Lexie? Lexie Hall shot that? She's one of our weakest shooters.

First line was up again. Annie tried to shake it off, but she couldn't. Things in the distance were blurry.

Naya sent a laser of a shot at her, and Annie couldn't stop it. It clanged off the goalpost and right into the net.

"Looks like there's a crack in The Wall today," Naya said with a laugh.

Annie didn't find her joke funny at all.

CHAPTER 5

NEW GLASSES

"How do they feel?" Annie's mom asked her.
They were sitting in the car, parked at the
curb outside East Grover Lake Middle School.
Around them, buses were arriving and kids
were filing into the school for another day
of class.

Annie fidgeted with the glasses perched
on her nose. She flipped down the car's
visor and looked at herself in the mirror.
The frames were thin, made to look like they

weren't even there. Which was exactly what she'd wanted.

"Weird," Annie answered. "They're giving me a headache."

"They'll just take some getting used to," her mom said. "Mine were the same way." Her mom was not wearing glasses now. In fact, she only wore them at night. Otherwise, she wore contacts.

"If you say so." Annie was not a fan of her newest fashion accessory, but she had to admit, she was relieved that the reason for her blurry vision was not something more severe. She could get used to wearing glasses. Contacts? Maybe not. She hated the idea of touching her eyeballs, or of sticking something in them every day.

She shuddered just thinking about it.

"You best get to class," her mom said.

Annie said goodbye, lowered her head, and merged with the throng of students entering the school.

She turned back to see her mom driving away. Then she stopped and peeled the glasses off her head.

"So much better," she said, rubbing her eyes.

"Whatcha got there?" Logan asked from behind her.

Annie, startled, dropped her new glasses.

"No!" She quickly scrambled to scoop them up before someone stepped on them. Thankfully, they were unharmed.

"Are those glasses?" Gabe asked. He and Logan stood watching her fumble with them.

"They're none of your business." Annie didn't know why she was hiding the glasses. Her friends were going to find out eventually. She just didn't want the whole school to know right away.

"They are," Logan said. "Did you just get them?"

Annie sighed. "Yes. Fine. I got glasses. Big whoop, okay."

The three kids began walking into school again, down a long hall toward their lockers. "It *is* a big whoop," Logan said. "How are you going to play hockey wearing glasses?"

"My optometrist—"

"Your what?!" Logan interrupted.

"My *eye doctor*—"

"Ah, gotcha."

"—said there's a pair of special sports goggles I can wear. She ordered me a pair, and I can pick them up after school tomorrow."

"Cool." Logan hiked his backpack up on his shoulder.

"Which is perfect, because we've got two big games coming up in a row, including the one against West Grover Lake, and I am *not* going to miss them."

"Let's see what they look like," Gabe said, nodding at the glasses.

Annie slid them on again. She tried hard to make them fit comfortably. They didn't, and she could practically feel the headache come thundering back.

Gabe smiled and said, "I think they look nice."

"Thanks," she said quietly. The trio split up, Gabe and Logan heading in one direction for their first class, Annie in the other. She needed to hit her locker before the bell rang.

That was when she saw Ben approaching from the other direction. His face scrunched up when he saw her.

"Hey, are you wearing glasses?" he asked.

Annie rolled her eyes. *Here we go again.*

That afternoon, she watched practice from the bench. She didn't have her new goggles yet, so she was wearing her new glasses.

Coach Cressman stood beside her as the team ran drills. It felt strange, sitting on the bench. She shoved her hands into the front pocket of her hooded sweatshirt. The letters EGL were emblazoned across the chest.

"Great work!" Coach Cressman shouted. "First line, let's try it again!"

Annie kept her eyes on Emma in the goal. She still looked slow. The first line was easily able to score a short-handed goal on her.

Coach Cressman cleared his throat, turning briefly away from the ice. Annie could see he was frustrated, but he yelled, "Keep at it, Emma!"

Annie looked behind her just in time to see Carter sit down in the bleachers.

He dropped his backpack beside him and rummaged inside it for a notebook and a paperback copy of *Huckleberry Finn*, which they were reading in American Literature class.

Unlike many kids in their class, Carter seemed genuinely excited to crack open the book. As he began to read, he glanced over and saw her.

He smiled and waved.

She waved back.

He pointed to his eyes, mouthed the words *Nice glasses*, and gave her a thumbs-up.

Annie could feel her cheeks flush with embarrassment. She mouthed *Thanks*, and then turned back to watch the action on the ice.

CHAPTER 6

A STOP AT SAL'S

Instead of going to practice the following afternoon, Annie rode with her mother so they could stop back at Dr. Rosen's. Annie had ordered some prescription sports goggles for when she was on the ice. Coach Cressman had given her the okay to miss practice. After all, he wanted his starting goalie back. And Annie was confident that she'd be back in top form once she had the sports goggles.

Dr. Rosen's office was located in a small brick building in downtown Grover Lake. The buildings were coated in a fresh layer of powdery snow, thanks to a flurry that had struck earlier that morning.

Annie knew the area well; Sal's Used Sporting Goods was right down the block. Sal's was one of her favorite places in the whole wide world. It was old, with shelves upon shelves of dusty merchandise, hidden treasures just waiting to be discovered. Its owner and namesake, Sal Horton, had a wonderful knack for knowing exactly what Annie and her friends needed, sometimes before they even knew it themselves.

Sure enough, as Annie stepped onto the snowy sidewalk in front Dr. Rosen's office, she saw Sal's burly figure standing under the orange awning of his store. He was wearing a red and-black plaid winter coat and a fur hat with flaps that covered his ears. Sal was shoveling a thin layer of snow that had fallen over the course of the day.

"Mom, I want to say hi to Sal before we go in," Annie said.

Her mother checked her watch. "Sure. We have a few minutes before Dr. Rosen is expecting us."

The two carefully walked along the sidewalk, snow crunching underfoot.

When Sal saw Annie approaching, he straightened up. A wide smile crossed his bearded face. "Why, hello there, Annie!" he said in his booming voice.

Even with her new glasses, and the headache that seemed to come with them, Annie couldn't help but smile back. Sal just had that affect on her.

"Hiya, Sal," she said.

Sal leaned on the shovel's wide handle and said, "I like your glasses."

"Thanks."

"How's the new season treating my favorite goaltender?"

She shook her head. "Not great."

"Oh, no. That's not what I like to hear. Why so glum?"

"We lost our first game."

Sal's smile faded. "Well, heck, Annie," he said. "It's just one game. I'm sure things will go better for you with your new glasses."

"Yeah, I suppose," she said.

"Good luck with the season," Sal said. "I'll try to catch a game when I can."

"Thanks, Sal." Annie and her mom shuffled off down the snowy sidewalk and back toward their car. Behind them came the sounds of Sal's shovel scraping against the concrete once more.

MELTDOWN

"All right," Annie said to herself, "let's see how these bad boys work."

She was sitting alone in the girls' locker room, in full uniform. The team had traveled to the neighboring town of Hillston, to face the home team Vipers. The rest of the Grizzlies had already suited up and were on the ice.

Annie held in her hands the sports goggles. They had black frames, with one thick strap that wrapped around the back of her head.

She slid the goggles over her tangle of curly brown hair, then placed them over her eyes, and adjusted them until they were snug.

"Whoa." She placed her hand in front of her. Everything looked crisp, all the way across the locker room. Annie went to join the rest of the team.

"Grizzlies!" *Clap! Clap!* "Grizzlies!" *Clap! Clap!*

The crowd was already riled up. Because Hillston was a short drive from Grover Lake, many Grizzlies fans, including Annie's whole family, were in attendance. As usual, her friends sat just above the bench.

"You ready?" Coach Cressman said, slapping her on the shoulder pad. Out on the ice, the team was taking practice shots at the open net.

"Ready to win, Coach."

"That's what I like to hear."

Annie skated onto the ice and took her place in front of the goal. The crowd noise swelled as she took a deep breath and clapped her gloved hands together. She was back, and it felt great.

That is, until she placed the mask over her head.

With the new goggles, the mask felt uncomfortable. Cumbersome, even. She tried hard to adjust the mask, to get it just right, but she couldn't quite figure it out.

Just play through it, she thought.

The Vipers, clad in yellow and green, stared down at her. Annie was positive their coach had heard about her accident and told his players to strike fast and strike hard. As vipers do.

The first lines took their places.

The ref dropped the puck.

Ruby Vogel came away with it, slicing it across the neutral zone to Naya. She brought it forward, dancing the puck back and forth with her stick. The Vipers defensive players hung back, waiting for the right moment. Ruby set up in front of the goal. When Naya fired a pass through the middle, it was easily intercepted.

The Vipers swung the puck to the wall, . where their center caught it and passed it up. As she did, she collided with Ruby, who was trying to steal the pass. The puck skittered

ahead, across the blue line, where the Vipers'
left wing gobbled it up.

As she brought the puck forward,
Annie found herself struggling again to see
the puck. Not because of her eyesight. It
was the combination of her mask with the
new goggles.

She wanted to rip the mask off.

The wing took a shot, and before Annie
could get her blocker up, the puck struck
her solidly in the chest guard. Even with
protection, the shot stung. The wind was
knocked from her lungs.

She couldn't rest, though. The Vipers
fiercely skated around the zone, snatching up
the puck. The Vipers' right wing slid a pass
along to the center, who lined up a slap shot
that whooshed through the air.

Annie's eyes grew wide.

Crack!

The puck hit her mask solidly, knocking her back, stunned. The Vipers' center recovered her own shot and flipped it in easily.

The Viper fans went nuts.

Annie tore the mask from her head.

"Hey, you okay?" Ruby asked as she skated up. Some of the other girls joined her.

It wasn't the first time Annie had taken a shot off the mask. Or the chest. Or an arm or a leg. Or pretty much anywhere.

It was, however, the first time she'd been completely freaked out by it. She just couldn't keep track of the puck. And that scared her.

She shook her head. "No," she said, peeling off the goggles, too. "No, I'm not."

She skated to the bench and saw the concerned look on Coach Cressman's face. "What's wrong?" he asked.

"I don't know," Annie said. There was a hitch in her voice. "Just . . . just send Emma in."

Annie sat down on the bench and threw her mask down.

What is wrong with me?

She could feel hot tears welling up in her eyes, mixing with sweat, stinging them. She clutched the sports goggles in her hands and forced back the tears. She couldn't let her teammates see her cry.

CHAPTER 8

GIFT FROM A FRIEND

On the ride home, Annie sat in the back seat of the car, not wanting to say a word. Her parents tried a couple of times to spark a conversation, to ask her exactly what had happened and why she'd vanished into the locker room. They gave up when they realized she wasn't going to answer them.

The Vipers had handed the Grizzlies their second loss in a row.

Great way to start a season, Annie thought. *Two games, two losses.*

It was late in the evening when they arrived home. The sun had dropped below the horizon, and hazy darkness had taken over the wintry landscape. Annie trudged through the house to her bedroom to sit alone in silence and think about what had happened earlier.

It didn't work. After less than ten minutes, she felt claustrophobic, like the walls of her bedroom were pushing in on her.

Arrggh! I need fresh air.

Annie grabbed her coat, tugged a stocking cap onto her head, and slipped out of the house.

Once outside, she pulled on a pair of gloves. Her breath clouded in front of her, and she shivered. With her head low, Annie began to walk through a snowdrift at the side of the garage. She was headed to the backyard. More specifically, she was headed for the tree house nestled in the big oak tree at the corner of their yard.

She and her dad had built it three summers ago. It was more for Olivia. Annie wasn't much of a tree house kind of kid, but she'd enjoyed spending time with her dad, using power tools and hammers and actually building something she was proud of.

Sections of two-by-four boards had been nailed into the tree trunk as steps. Annie wiped snow from the lowest ones and began to climb. She swept them off as she went.

The inside of the tree house was bare, except for a few stray toys.

Annie sat on the cold wood floor, drawing up her knees and wrapping her arms tightly around her legs. She didn't know exactly what she was doing there. It just felt . . . *right*. She recalled once, the winter after the tree house had been built, when she had been so furious with her parents about something, she'd packed a bag and stormed out of the house, saying she was running away. Her plan had been to walk to Ben's house and stay there. Instead, she'd climbed up to the tree house.

She'd lasted 15 minutes that time before going back inside to warm up.

Annie thought about the hockey game, about how it felt to have fear washing over her, nearly drowning her. She hated her new glasses and goggles, and how they made her feel like she'd never be able to play hockey again.

Then she heard a soft shushing sound, like someone walking through snow.

She held her breath and waited.

"Annie?"

Her dad, she would have expected. Her mom, possible, but doubtful. But there was no way she expected . . .

"Carter?"

Annie leaned out one of the tree house's crudely shaped windows. Sure enough, Carter Cressman stood looking up at her. He wore a bulging backpack, as if he'd left school with every one of his textbooks in tow.

"Uh, can I come up?" he asked.

"Sure." Annie watched as he fumbled for the first rung of her makeshift ladder. He wasn't wearing gloves, and she could only imagine how cold his fingers must have been.

He grunted and strained as he hauled himself up the ladder. With a *thump*, he dropped his backpack and sat beside her.

"Hey," he said.

"Hey."

"Nice view. You can really see, uh, your roof from up here."

A hint of a smile flickered across Annie's face.

"So how are you feeling?" he asked.

She shrugged. "I don't know. Weird."

"Because of the glasses?"

"Yeah, I guess. I've never doubled myself or my goaltending before. It scared me."

"When I was, like, ten, I was at this skatepark. It had the coolest vert ramp. I bet my friend I could do a 360 off of it. I went up the ramp, high into the air, and nailed it."

"Yeah?"

"Yeah. Right up until I hit the ramp. With my face." He lifted his chin. A thin, white scar that Annie had never seen before ran the length of it. "Wound up with eight stitches."

"Ouch. Let me guess. You haven't ridden a skateboard since."

"I ride all the time." Pause. "It's all about finding a way to conquer your fear. Starting with that stupid broken mask of yours."

Carter reached for his backpack and unzipped it. From inside, he withdrew a hockey mask, red with white trim and bars.

"Wait a minute . . . ," Annie whispered.

"I got it at Sal's," Carter said, hefting the mask. "I wanted to give it to you before the game against West Grover Lake. Guess I shouldn't have waited."

He handed the mask over to Annie. It was lightweight but a bit larger than the one she had been using. On one side was a small white maple leaf.

"Why is the Canadian flag on it?" she asked.

"Because it used to belong to Shannon Szabados."

"Get out." Annie's breath caught in her throat. Szabados was one of Annie's heroes. She was the only two-time Olympic gold medalist goaltender.

"She used to practice in it," Carter added. "At least that's what Sal told me."

Annie had watched every game that Szabados had played in during the Olympics. In fact, she pretty much knew the 2010 gold-medal game—in which Szabados and the

Canadians shut out the Americans 2-0—by heart. People called it one of the greatest goaltending performances in the history of the game.

"I didn't tell him, but Sal knew it was for you," Carter said.

"That's Sal for you." Annie smiled, and for the first time since she'd gotten glasses, she felt hopeful, as if she could take the ice again. Szabados never let anything get in the way of her success. She had helped beat one of the world's best women's hockey teams. She was now playing in a men's hockey league, against bigger and stronger players. If Szabados can succeed against those odds, Annie felt she should not let something minor like having to wear glasses defeat her.

Annie ran her fingers along the mask and then slid it over her head. "A perfect fit," she said. "Thanks, Carter."

Then, before she realized what she was doing, she reached over and hugged him. She'd never been so bold before.

When they parted, Carter whispered, "So, seriously, what are you doing up here? It's freezing."

Annie laughed. "I have no idea," she said.

She shed the mask, and together, they climbed down out of the tree house.

CHAPTER 9

CONQUER YOUR FEARS

Like every sports matchup between the town's rival schools, the game against the West Grover Lake Hornets was, in a word, epic. Throngs of people poured into the tiny ice rink, crowding both sides of the bleachers in either Grizzlies red and brown or Hornets yellow and blue.

Annie was peeking out the door of the locker room at the mass of cheering fans. She spied her friends in their usual spot. This time, even Carter was wearing one of Logan's ridiculous bear hats. Her family sat nearby, too, clapping along to the music echoing through the rink, courtesy of the East Grover Lake Pep Band.

"I don't have a big speech planned," Coach Cressman growled. "Because you don't need it. You just need to be hungry. To fight off fear and play the game like it's meant to be played: with heart."

Ruby Vogel whooped and slapped her stick against the nearest locker. Other players joined in.

"On three!" Coach Cressman shouted. "One! Two! *Three!*"

"Go Grizzlies!" the entire team roared.

They took the ice, a frenzied squad of pumped-up girls. Annie looked up at Carter and twirled the mask for him. He laughed. Logan eyed him quizzically.

When Annie took the ice, sports goggles over her eyes, mask in hand, she felt a twinge of fear twist in her stomach. It was fleeting, but it was there. She pushed it away, didn't let it get its claws into her. Instead, she slid the mask that had once belonged to Shannon Szabados over her head. She felt powerful, like a knight in shining armor protecting her castle from hordes of monsters.

After the two teams warmed up and introductions were made, Ruby Vogel took center ice opposite the Hornets' Jill O'Connell.

Tweet!

The ref dropped the puck.

Ruby hacked at the face-off, clashing with Jill. The Hornets' center won, passing the puck to the left wing, who skated furiously into the zone.

"Be aggressive!" she heard the Hornets' coach shout over the din of the crowd.

The wing slapped the puck back to the center, who carved right up the middle. Annie saw her coming and felt the fear start to bubble up again.

Focus, Annie! she told herself. *FOCUS!*

She saw the puck crisply, and kept her eyes on it as Jill unleashed a powerful shot that sliced through the air, right at Annie's head.

Thwack!

It struck her glove, and Annie squeezed tight.

The ref blew the whistle, stopping play.

"Great save, Wall," Ruby said as she skated past. "Good to have you back."

The first period was a blur of action, as both teams attacked their respective zones. Annie had never had so many shots on goal in one period of play. She blocked, grabbed, and deflected each attempt.

In the second period, the Grizzlies almost notched their first goal, off a deflection by Lexie Hall. The third-line wing shoveled the puck into the air, just past the outstretched glove of the Hornets' goalie. Unfortunately, it clanged off the crossbar, giving the goaltender a chance to smother it with her gloves.

At the start of the third period, Annie glanced up at the scoreboard. It was still 0-0.

Two big, fat goose eggs, she thought.

"Keep it up, Annie!" she heard Gabe shout from the bleachers.

"You can do it!" Carter added.

Any fear or hesitation she had about the new mask and sports goggles had disappeared. She was as focused as a laser. When the Hornets threatened late in the game, Annie's instincts took over. Jill O'Connell brought the puck around, passing it off to the right wing. The wing slapped a shot, and Annie deflected it with her blocker. Jill was there for the rebound, flipping a wrist shot toward the corner of the goal. Annie, her back turned from the action, spun and leaped through the air. She thrust her stick out. The puck glanced off it, mere inches from the red line.

The Hornet center was there for her own rebound, though. She swung. Annie dove.

The puck connected with her new helmet. It made her ears ring. Annie didn't have time to think about that, though. She spied the puck bouncing off the ice and quickly leaped atop it.

Tweet!

"Face-off!" the ref shouted.

Annie staggered to her feet. She shook her head to clear it.

"You all right, Wall?" Ruby asked.

Annie smiled. "Peachy."

The Grizzlies were able to clear the puck from the zone on the ensuing face-off, but they were unable to score.

When the final buzzer sounded, the score was still 0-0.

CHAPTER 10

OVERTIME

Sudden death overtime. Annie couldn't think of a more frightening term in sports. It *did* have the word *death* in it, after all. There was no room for error. The first team to score won the game.

Annie and the Grizzlies stood near the bench. They were completely exhausted. Annie had her mask off, her goggles pulled up onto her sweaty forehead. The game had been fast-paced, unrelenting. It was brutal, and they were all feeling the strain.

"I know it's been tough," Coach Cressman said. "You're going to have to dig deep, though. Give just a little more."

The refs blew their whistles, and Annie skated back out to the goal. She took a deep breath, let it out slowly, and then lowered her goggles and mask.

The two teams picked up where they left off. Annie had never seen the Grizzlies skate with such determination and passion. It was exhilarating. Ruby won the face-off and snaked into the zone untouched. She passed across to Naya, who quickly tried to force a shot.

The goalie deflected it, and the puck bounced off the board, into the zone . . .

. . . and right to a speeding Jill O'Connell.

She broke through the defensive players and came straight at Annie. It was one-on-one, Annie against Jill. Annie crouched down, waiting for the shot . . .

This is it, she thought.

Jill faked left, carved right, and fired a shot at the corner of the goal.

Annie, her eyes on the puck, wasn't fooled.

She plucked the shot out of the air easily.

Tweet!

"Great save, Annie!" her friends shouted in unison from the bleachers.

The two teams lined up in the circle to Annie's left. As Ruby looked over to her, Annie said, "Finish this thing, will ya?"

71

Ruby smiled and winked.

The puck dropped, and Ruby passed it off to Piper. Piper slid it over to Britney, who spied an open Heidi cutting across the middle. Heidi took the pass and skated into the Hornets' zone.

The two defensive players for the Hornets swarmed her. Neither of them saw Ruby Vogel flying down the left side of the rink.

Heidi did, though.

Just as the defensive players reached her, Heidi flipped the puck across to the wide-open center.

Ruby caught it in stride. She came to a quick stop, spraying ice from both skates. She brought back her stick and swung down hard.

The puck sailed through the air so fast even Annie had trouble following it.

It struck the back of the net.

The sirens wailed. The red lights flashed. The crowd roared.

Annie dropped to her knees, exhausted. *We did it!* she thought.

The rest of the Grizzlies poured off the bench to join the celebration on the ice.

"Great win!" Coach slapped each player on the helmet as they passed him.

Annie removed her mask and mouth guard. She couldn't wait to celebrate with her team. First, though, she skated over toward the bench, to the spot where her friends were jumping up and down and offering each other high fives.

When they saw her, Ben called out, "Annie! That was amazing!"

"Best hockey game I've ever seen!" Logan added.

Annie smiled. She held the mask up, looked at Carter, and quietly said, "Thanks."

He nodded and smiled back.

With that, feeling on top of the world, her heart soaring high, Annie joined the other Grizzlies at center ice for a victory lap around the rink.

THE END

ABOUT THE AUTHOR

Brandon Terrell is a Saint Paul-based writer. He is the author of numerous children's books, including picture books, chapter books, and graphic novels. When not hunched over his laptop, Brandon enjoys watching movies and television, reading, baseball, and spending every spare moment with his wife and their two children.

ABOUT THE HOCKEY STAR

Shannon Szabados was a hero of both the 2010 and 2014 Winter Olympics. She helped Canada's women's hockey team win gold medals. After the 2014 Olympics, she played in the Southern Professional Hockey League (SPHL) on a men's minor league team.

Position: Goaltender

National Team: Canada

Olympic Medals: 2 gold

THINK ABOUT IT

1. Imagine that you were Annie. How do you think you would have reacted against the Vipers after getting hit by the puck several times? Would you have skated off the ice like she did or would you have done something different?

2. Read another Game On! story. Compare the roles Annie plays in the two stories. In *Eyes on the Puck*, she needs help regaining her confidence goaltending. Is this different from or similar to what she does in the other story? Use examples from the two stories to explain your answer.

3. Have you ever struggled like Annie when doing something that you normally do well? What was the activity? Why did you struggle? And how did you overcome your difficulties?

WRITE ABOUT IT

1. Carter gives Annie a new mask in hopes of helping her regain her confidence. Has anyone ever helped you overcome a fear? Write down what that person did or said to help you, and what happened the next time you had to face your fear.

2. Annie's nickname on her hockey team is The Wall. Do you have a fun nickname? Write a story about how you earned it.

3. Annie has a close-knit group of friends: Logan, Ben, and Gabe. Do you have a bunch of friends you hang out with a lot? Write about what you like to do together. Do you have similar interests like sports or video games?

GET YOUR GAME ON!

Read more about Annie and her friends as they get their game on.

Pass for the Basket
When a new transfer student takes away the spotlight, Ben Mason is frustrated with his role on the basketball team. Will Ben be able to learn the true meaning of leadership?

Race Down the Slopes
Blinded by a crush, Gabe Santiago accepts an invitation to join the ski team even though he has never skied slalom before. Will a pair of goggles from Sal's Used Sporting Goods prove to be Gabe's lucky charm?

Strike Out the Side
Logan Parrish has a great fastball, but hitters are starting to figure him out. After a devastating loss, Logan goes searching for a new pitch. Will it be enough to help Logan in the big game?